# TROVE OF THOUGHTS

## THE MODERN DOCTOR FAUSTUS AND OTHER STORIES - SECTION I

AF439229

### SURUR PRAKASH BHARADWAJ

Copyright © Surur Prakash Bharadwaj
All Rights Reserved.

This book has been self-published with all reasonable efforts taken to make the material error-free by the author. No part of this book shall be used, reproduced in any manner whatsoever without written permission from the author, except in the case of brief quotations embodied in critical articles and reviews.

The Author of this book is solely responsible and liable for its content including but not limited to the views, representations, descriptions, statements, information, opinions and references ["Content"]. The Content of this book shall not constitute or be construed or deemed to reflect the opinion or expression of the Publisher or Editor. Neither the Publisher nor Editor endorse or approve the Content of this book or guarantee the reliability, accuracy or completeness of the Content published herein and do not make any representations or warranties of any kind, express or implied, including but not limited to the implied warranties of merchantability, fitness for a particular purpose. The Publisher and Editor shall not be liable whatsoever for any errors, omissions, whether such errors or omissions result from negligence, accident, or any other cause or claims for loss or damages of any kind, including without limitation, indirect or consequential loss or damage arising out of use, inability to use, or about the reliability, accuracy or sufficiency of the information contained in this book.

Made with ❤ on the Notion Press Platform
www.notionpress.com

*To My Padre,*

*Pandit Shree Prakash Chandra Bal Sundar Sharma,*

Enter Caption

I ask your benevolent bliss in my schemes

And, the light you have graced from There I Shall Begin

# Contents

# Acknowledgements

This is hereby the section of the extraordinary debt to Their wisdom, Shri Ganesh, Lakshmi Narayan, Gauri Shankar, Saraswati, Hanuman and Shani Maharaj, and all the other Gods and Goddesses in this world who created me with such a significant gift and also blessed me with virtue and great responsibilities. I would call upon my speech to the Great Grand Father, Pandit Daulat Ram Sharma, and guardians who blessed me with nobility, My Maternal and Paternal Grandparents, Pratima Chaturvedi, Bipin Parashar, Panditain Bimla Devi, Pandit Bal Sundar Daulat Ram Sharma respectively. My Mother and Father, Panditain Sair Prakash Sharma and Pandit Prakash Chandra Bal Sundar Sharma loved me and rendered all their support and always motivated me in my thoughts and decisions. They are my lucky charm and my life. My two chucklesome sisters, Suhi and Ruhi Prakash Bharadwaj who always laughed with me and acted as the caretakers in my life, and My Young kinsperson, Pandit Surup Prakash Sharma as my brother who acted as the helping hand in my quirky struggles. My family is the backbone of my every area of struggle.

Furthermore, I would show up my sense of obligation to the dearest Teachers and Professors from the heydays of my school, Mrs. Elizabeth Francis, Mrs. Nenu Arackel, Mrs. Irin, Mrs. Shakti Thakur, Mrs. Shilpa Bhatnagar, Mrs. Ravika, Mrs. Ritika Sagar, Mrs. Loveleen Kaur, Mrs. Gauri, Mrs. Shama Sherwani, Rev. Sr. Cecile, Rev. Fr. Cancius Ligoure, Rev. Fr. Susai Manikum, Mr. Cosmos, Mr. Jason Chaku, Mr. Sunil Jose, Mr.Anoop Mathur who watered the seed of my curiosity and brilliance and, My wonderful Professors, Dr. Kusum Lata, Mrs. Kanchan Mohindra, Dr. Seema Mathur, Mrs. Mini Gill, Dr. Ipshita Nath, Mr. Rajnikant, Dr. Minu Kashyap, Dr. Abhishek Tiwari, Dr. Himani Sharma, and others who always appreciated my faith in artistic values and motivated me in the narrative path.

And, also my companions and friends who always wanted to see my writings in published form, who always appreciated my art, Juliana Anjos, Dailane Melowe, Neelam Rajput, Shivani Karki Aakansha Nautiyal, Stephen John, Rahul Khandelwal, Madhvendra "THE MADDY" Singh, Luiz Antonio Barbara Junior, Cliff Martin, Nelson David, Anant Mishra, Steve & Sylvester Jude Williams, Faraz Ahmed, Nitin Panwar, Hemant Kumar, Bhuvan Verma, Aayush Gupta, Deepak Singh, and others who cheered me and buck up my strengths and knowledge into valuing arts and rhetoric. Also, they admired my writings as well as my consistency in workmanship.

A Special gesture to my elders, Gulnar and Ratan Tawadia, Fatima Khan Pathan, and Achynt Tryambak Padwal (Appa) as my success is incomplete without their blessings.

Lastly, all my lovely students whom I had taught also boosted my spirit and motivated my enthusiasm.

# Epigraph

"The most dangerous action of Modern Aesthetics is having partial knowledge of anything which leads our consciousness to the dark alleys of misfortune where we pretend to be legitimate but actually, we grope to find the missing pieces of wisdom."

- SURUR PRAKASH BHARADWAJ

# THE MODERN DOCTOR FAUSTUS

## *I*

The age-long history of The Ragwort Castle with ruins as a symbol of defeat and creepers hugging the ashed walls tightly for years now; with eerie cries of a young maiden rumored to be the residing place of The Dullahan, in the high command of the Great Devil. The demon who crawls from South to West, North to East claiming souls every night, parks his Death Chariot, holding his skull as a suitcase in hand. Everything seems quiet for a moment. His life was oscillating between parallels of thoughts to do or not to do. The castle was barren for a while as the air moves through the holes while taking spiders to the front door. The place sounds appealing to the omens. Their walls were aligned into bricks with chambers and have circular staircases. The rooms were quiet and murky with no furniture. Someone broke the silence when the front door opened with a crank voice. The Doctor came to the castle once again and started glancing at the ground. He was waiting for a moment to happen, the tattow on his nape reflects a merry suicidal scene; a girl is smiling, swinging and a man is hanging from the rope of her swing. Is he punished? No one knows.

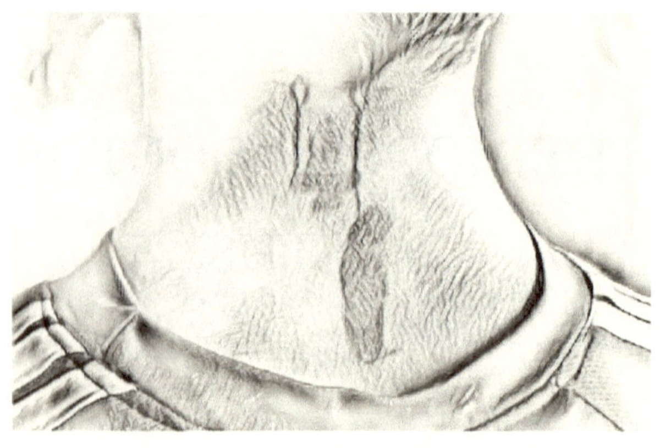

Modern Faustus's Nape tattow

The doctor was flabbergasted in his thoughts and broke the ornamented plate to cut the silence at Ragwort. No one bothered him except the Dullahan. The doctor had practiced philosophy, astrology, law, literature, religion, and even medicine but found necromancy his favorite anecdote. He was known to every field but still parched upon the underworld affairs with the motive to get his wife back from the dimensions of death. He walked every possible path but all turned towards the Fairy Pools.

"O Sheelin! Where have you gone, I don't believe in your departure. Every night at the shores of Fairy Pool, Selkies come and dance but my eyes are in longing for you which fails to identify you among the crowd. Have you forgotten that Selkies are the saviors for drowning humans? I am drowning in the Sea of Sorrow much deeper than the Great Seas on Earth, Why don't you save me from drowning?"

Once again he was in the Ragwort Castle. On his very place, he walked along the smelled alley which was connected to the room with no window. He had always a stick covered with a cloth that

was tied up with metal strings. The room sits in utter silence with no oxygen to breathe. The doctor was carrying Grand Grimoire and books of Nicolas Flamel, Thomas Crofton Croker, and Bernard Trevisan from whom he took inspiration. Eerie cries of a young maiden entered into his ear caves but he didn't bother as those cries were not of Sheelin and nor of the Demon. He then started practicing magic. With the stick coated in a cloth was wet with his blood of him and the urine of spiders. He utters the spell,
"Seeth it until it comes to blackness, which will be thought Evil. But wouldest thou know what is meant by this man, that taketh the Sword? It signifies that thou must cut off the head of the Crow, that is to say, of the man clothed in divers Colours, which is on his knees."
The doctor wiped his sweat and sat momentarily while watching the stick with patience. Thinking of his wife who had left him a long back ago made him the circumstances of activities. He started this magic as the only medium left which can claim back her wife.
"Now I realized why God is not helping me, neither to heal my sorrow nor to return my Sheelin from his dimension. God has a long rivalry with the Fallen Angels, God will not help them. Tis way I found the cure and the whereabouts of a High Ranked Official in The Pandemonium of The Mighty Leader of Fallen Angels. The Selkies are also Fallen Angels and I know your name means the same. Mighty Lucifer will bestow me. Things take time to happen and this sorrow has to be carried till then, I heard and will see that Devil will answer far sooner than the God."


"Tis wizardry will make Tis happen."


The Dullahan reached Ragwort after his services and sits on his throne in between the boiling blood and magma. He was hornless with his eyes on the upward state. He was happy to receive signals from his ardent new follower.

The doctor started his next ritual this day.
" Don't you do this Sir! Don't ignore my cries, your aftermath will be devastating." The eerie sobbing cries of the maiden.
This time he heard something from that young maiden who always cries but that sounds mundane to him. He moved the next door to a closed alley towards the stairs. Those stairs were almost on the back of the mansion and were old enough. The doctor was stepping on the narrow stairs to the roof of the building. There he began collecting ingredients for the magic. Makes a Triangle with blood on the wall, took the stick, cut the spiders and rats and soaked the cloth in their blood, and offered their flesh to his chosen demon. Then, he picked the barrette of his wife and chopped his 'Bys Kres' placed it in between the band, and lastly offered all the sacrificial pieces of stuff to the Dullahan. That moment he earned the attention of The Dullahan, his signals have reached. The demon picked the barrette in his hands and came closer to it for listening to the signals. Every chopped piece of Doctor's Bys Kres narrated his entire story wrapped in sorrows. Dullahan Approved his desires and marked him in his companionship.

## *II*

Days passed and Doctor's despair has no cure yet.
"Welcome again Doctor!"
"Who is that? Are you a slave to Dullahan? I know you came to deliver a message."
"Yes Yes! Slave to Dullahan, the path you have taken will lead you to join me soon."
"I will walk in any possible or impossible direction which leads me to the hope of getting my Sheelin back."
Her guffaws broke the silence in The Ragwort and also the hopes

of Doctor. Slowly it turned into the sobbing cries that Doctor usually hears in the castle.

" I get it now. You are that young maiden who always cries. You always tried to pass your emotional contagion to others." - Doctor's taunting gestures were crystal clear.

"Let me tell you my journey, may you grasp some essence from it and it may change your aftermath. I was an invalid and sickly child to The 11th Marquess Finley O' Conner and Marchioness Maeve O' Conner of Ragwort, BerylLann. My family was the richest among the areas of the neighborhood and my Father's benevolent behavior created a healthy and joyful atmosphere in the area. He always organized an annual festival and invite all the people; rich or poor, peasants or herders. We called it - 'The Rince ag Ragwort', where people cherish the season together, and dance at the riverside near our castle."

"This doesn't excite me though, now you will start with your fancy dresses and kinds of stuff of delicacy. You should barf out the pain if you have any or if you are just making up a lamentable affair for me to pity and listen." Doctor's sudden rudeness remarked.

"Introduction is necessary to mark all the key figures and events."

"I didn't find any keys which are concerned with my closed locks."

"You will be in the pack of slaves soon, you will beg for an apology for not listening before. Then you will find all sorts of logic and keys for your closed locks but then keys were of no use for doors at the dead end."

"The key to my door will open right in front of My Dear Sheelin. You sob day in and day out but never understood the essence of sobbing on never-ending pain."

*III*

The ritual was still unanswered by The Dullahan. The doctor
stood up, his frustration is now at heights,
"I am calling you for a long time when will you come .....What's
lacking in my magic"

First encounter with The Demon


"She will be in your lap." The devil replied from behind and as
soon as Doctor turned back to see him, he disappeared.

"Don't you dare disappear now? Come forward....Aa......At...At
least tell me when she will come."

The devil grabbed his throat from behind and poured his message
into his ears,

"Why do you want your wife, she left the ground already and if
you want her back, just do as I say, My Son. It's very simple for a
Man like you who doesn't fear anything and had crossed all

boundaries...."

The doctor nodded his head and began doing so. He climbed to the pinnacle of the Melow Castle and then he twisted his head and severed his head from his torso in the Name of the Devil. The demon carried the lifeless body of the Doctor on his shoulder and took him into the labyrinth seated below the castle. He dropped him on the table and started chanting the omens and made him his slave. The soul of the doctor began reacting to his master, ticking the drop of blood on his forehead, and stood up. What he saw was the chaos in front of him, standing there examining his condition but reluctant. He was now the headless devil. Serving him and massaging his knees and legs. The devil grabbed him while scolding and ordering him to massage more smoothly and nicely. The doctor was tormented sitting in with no emotions and remembering his before life with a smile and feel. What he had done? Was there any logic in love or black magic? He had blasphemed God and this modern Faustus was never warned by God or he did in a way? Answers lie in conscience.

"O My foolish yet knowledgable Doctor! You made everything to get your dead wife back, defied all the ways, and submitted your will against The Devil but your Dead eyes full of Desires made you choose the devil and desire before all. You have forgotten the fate that you signed for yourself. You were a fool to forget the fact that you will not get your wife through this, nor you will get her ever... You will serve the devil forever as many others did and will do, this queue of humans in seek of shortcut will always increase."

*To the person whom you feel as your life, you love them a lot and you should cherish the mementos of your loved ones because once a person is gone, they will not return whatsoever your conditions are or whatever you do to summon them back.*

# FALSE FAITH

## *I*

"God, grant me and support my matters, I will oblate you... Please this time, please this time."

Rajesh was on his way to his examinations when he visited the temple early in the morning. He was confused and thrilled at the same time. Thanked God and asked for blessings. A Priest was sitting beside Mahadev and watching everything with his keen eyes. Rajesh touched his feet and asked for the Nector of God's Feet and said,

"May God me in passing my examination, Bless me, O Priest."

While offering the Nector of God's Feet, the Priest said to him,

"There will be no need for you to visit the temple again." and turned his head. Rajesh ignored his statement and went outside the temple, heading towards the examination center. The Examination center was overcrowded and Rajesh thought that "Maybe I got here late certainly." In a moment, he checked the time on his phone and realized he was not late yet but then with his next step, he was feeling unconscious and with no support fell on the side of the car.......

"He might not be the customer, I guess."

"Let's take him into our custody."

The two policemen were fussing while watching the customer nearby by a local shop and walked to him. The customer was asking for a pack of snacks from the shopkeeper and was denied when the shopkeeper asked for the money. He with his arrogant attitude rebuked him,

"Why will I pay you, you will be fired if you ask...I am a policeman working in civil dress, be within your limits alright? I have taken just a 10 rupee snack, shame on you! this is my right as we are

serving you and the people like you...."
As he was remarking on his deeds, the two policemen called him up from behind and for his help sarcastically. He opened the pack of snacks and started munching while listening to the policemen, "First of all, tell us how do you know policemen were patrolling?" asked one policeman.

"What's a stupid question, I am the real policeman working in a civil dress not just like you who are misguiding," said Ranga.

"Don't talk rubbish! you should know the consequences. Don't make words with me. I will empty this snack in your mouth with the packing. Listening"

"Master, are you the real policeman?"

"Yes!!"

"How can I believe you?"

"We will drive you to the police station then you will know simply." said another policeman

"Please master, I am a timid man, I was joking.......how can I help you? Have the snack...." said Ranga.

"As I am a public servant, not a waiter."

The second policeman interrupted them and snatched his snack and said,

"How can I say no to food? Just give it."

"How can you say this? Doing party. You fool!" said in frustration by the first policeman.

They both changed the topic and ordered Ranga to a task of concern,

"There is work for you as you have been dealing with this small area for a time. You have to inform us about the murders which were happening here for a couple of days. Who is the culprit, if you can find it out, inform me as earliest as you can....got it."

"Gotcha!.....but how can you say fact with utmost surety that the reason for these incidents is the murders...You are talking about that accident on the road that was natural sir.....And, secondly, the

boy who fell from his roof just slipped by mistake or may have committed suicide..... And, if you are asking for the uncle who lives behind this particular street, he got a heart attack that was not a murder...Wait I will tell you what is not known to you one boy when he was on the road nearby an examination center also died due to unconsciousness."
"Whatttttt that's so."
"This is quite good, after having the 10 rupee snack, we are having 500 rupees talks. " said in laughter by the second policeman.
"Don't poke your nose in other matters, just make sure to complete the task which I just dictated to you, Right."
"Thank you, sir."

Priest giving Nector of God's Feet to The Policeman


Priest gives Nector of God's Feet to The Policeman

Both the policemen were patrolling again and one of them was the first to reach the temple and thought to visit for worshipping. He alighted his boots and entered. They offered to Mahadev and asked the priest sitting beside them for the Nector of God's Feet. The Priest offered him the Nector of God's Feet and the policeman walked off. At the temple gates, he was feeling drowsy, his head shaking in a puzzle and he fell off on the road in front of the temple gates. The second policeman saw him from afar and ran to check what's just happened to him.

"Doctor, Is everything fine, is anything to be afraid of?"

"Well everything is alright, it's so hailing that you bring him to the hospital on time or else he should have suffered more.

"What's the matter?"

"Listen, he got poisoned."

"Oh! See I know the reason might be that he has consumed the bad ill cooked food on the streets as he is always hungry."

"This type of poisoning seriously, how can you say this? Who made you the policeman.....By the way, he got Datura poisoning."


## II


"Har Har Mahadev" the Priest chanted peacefully.

"I have enjoyed this game, O Priest." said the policeman.

The priest turned back and saw the policeman behind him and was listening to him,

"God will always listen to their true followers, pardon me I had visited you that day just because of this...."

"Say in elaboration my dear, what you are trying to say....."

"You are not aware that policemen are patrolling in civil dress and what are they in search, will tell you in a second.....These days we have witnessed so many murders and deaths if those were suicides or, accidents. We found that Datura intoxication was the reason behind all the deaths in the neighborhood, they were not of natural circumstances. For an instance, take Rajesh who was there in this temple in the early morning and died due to intoxication on the road you made me your other victim but Mahadev has blessed me and saved my life. That day when I came to the temple you offered me Nector of God's Feet and I was taken ill, there I got the information that I was poisoned by Datura and I realized that I was on fasting that day - 'Nirjala Ekadashi', the only thing I consumed was Nector of God's Feet which you offered me because it can be taken during the fast."

"Can you proof this!!!"

"God made you caught, he's not with you as you defied the teachings of God. You are under arrest and your Nector of God's Feet will be into laboratory testing."

Priest confessing out


Priest confessing out

"Ok, I'm agreed, allow me for once to take shelter on His feet, as I have achieved whatsoever I aimed. By His Grace, I removed as many atheists from this society as I can, those who perform rituals for their benefits or to establish a societal image are indeed in need of a Last Lesson."
The priest turned to Mahadev, joined his hands, and worshipped. And then suddenly with a quick movement, he took the Nector of God's Feet and swallowed in one go, meeting his demise thereafter.

*The religious teaching which we own and seeks them
has to be significantly correct and if someone will
get the lessons of wisdom through the wrong medium
or things then that man can be a criminal in mere
future.*

# MRS. DULCET SILVA

*I*

"Take this madam, have a tea.........and say your matter in elaboration because you are under arrest with proof as we have found you supplying drugs...Are you aware of?...... So tell me frankly, you will be behind the bars. No one can save you but tell me all the matters that will help you in serving less punishment."

"Drugs, what are you talking about...How can you say this?"

"Just now half n hour before we have arrested you with certifications. And your unconscious state was also because of these drugs. I know the matter if you are supplying there is a possibility that you are taking them too....."

"No no"

"You are new to this locality and you have started this peddler's job. From where you were handling this business before?"

" No no, cops... You are taking me wrong......I am not getting what is happening and what are you saying......Also, how am I here actually I was having a cup of tea along with Mrs. Dulcet Silva and I don't know, I don't know, how I came here.....I am getting back my memories...I was sipping tea with her and now having the sort with you too......What's happening to me, I am not getting it."

"Ok, so you will not open your mouth. Fine, now stay behind the bars till further notice."

"No please I haven't done anything please listen...... Please."

**Three hours ago - Before the Arrest**

"Hello Aunt"

"Who are you?"

"I have shifted here these days...Your new neighbor.....I have listened from people around the building from guards, watchmen, and neighbors that the taste of your tea is mesmerizing. So, I thought to meet you and we will have a small get-together."

"Oh! Great most welcome, you have thought right."

She came inside and sat on the chair. Aunt moved into the kitchen and started preparing the tea. She poured the milk into the boiling tea leaves and arranged two glasses with a sugar cube each in them.

"You have decorated your table so well, you have good taste." She interrupted her while sitting on the chair.

"Yaa, I have a keen interest in interior designing, and my husband too...."

"Oh, I see that's the reason your house is full of decoratives,"

"Thank you"

"Oh! We should talk at least......Tea is less important than our conversations."

"Just coming in a while as the tea has already prepared...Now we can engage."

She poured the tea into two glasses and stirred one of the glasses with a silver spoon and offer the stirred glass to her neighbor,

"Why there's a spoon in my glass not in yours? You don't take sugar, right?"

"Yes, I don't entertain sugar, it is not to my taste. Same with my husband also."

"The color of the tea is so vibrant...I will now have it."

"Yes, liked it."

"Yes, tea is so good...Thank you for this."

"Now you know why all the people in the building loved the taste."

"Yaa...Yaa, you have a great taste in your tea."

Nola and Mrs. Dulcet

"Thank you......So what are you doing in your profession?"

"I had completed my college and got a placement here in his town. So, I will be doing my job here, in need of a nice place, and found it here besides yours."

"So that's great we can meet frequently."

"Yes right, I shifted here two days before and by the way what do you for living?"

" I am a housewife and sometimes I help my husband in his work."

"Oh we are so stupid, we are taking like continue but we haven't asked each other's name."

" My name is Mrs. Dulcet Silva and yours?"

"NOLA"

"Such a good name."

"Thank you."


## II


"Who are you?" Someone was at the door.

"I have shifted here today and I heard the appreciation of you and your tea."

"Oh! Welcome in house and have a seat."

Mrs. Dulcet preparing Tea

Mrs. Dulcet Silva prepared the tea in two glasses and offered him.

"Have it, sir"

"How can I be the sir, I have shifted here today."

They both shared the same laughter as they knew each other before and started talking,

"Cheers, our business never stops it will remain...I have the police dress and we have snared her in this matter. I have trapped her by giving her drugs and also demanded money for compensation. We will share this money in between and take care of this to run our business slowly until and unless the next neighbors will not be shifting."

"Ok, I will take care of this."

"You have enough tea drugs or not."

"Yes, I have enough."

"Take care of this thing, this time she was shivering in pain...Maybe she was not healthy or maybe you have her in more portions.....Use while taking care, it is costly though."

"Ok, I will take care."

Mrs. Dulcet Silva put the tea drugs in her glass. She sprinkles two pinches and stirs that with a spoon.

"Have a sip or this also contain it......." Her husband laughed sarcastically.

*If you are an innocent and amiable person, it does not mean that either person is also the mirror of your gesture. It is not wrong on your part that you are inviting offers out of your circles but still, unless you will get to know the status of the person, never consider them a kind-hearted human.*

# THIRST ON A ARID HURST

*I*

A Wanderer carelessly carrying a bag full of worthlessness. He was dancing from the leaves to the trees as if something was there for him. His hair was shabby into difficulties and his clothes showed the pangs of his past. Scratching his head, he was strolling through the grass in search of something of his desires. Picked up something as hope to him after realizing that he had hand-picked the box of medicine. The medicine strip couldn't heal him completely which shows that he was baffled with outraged physical and emotional motivates. He walked alone and along the downlines, walking barefoot and waking his hopes. He was glancing his eyes through air and spaces, writhing with scorching heat found nothing. He started panting and wanted to quench his dry throat. He started moving again and searching with dejection as everything was rejecting him and his presence. Suddenly, he brooded over the sight of a water bottle nearby and a pile of filth that seemed like dried leaves from a distance but was garbage. The wanderer took the moment into his hand and picked up the trophy of his day. He was forcing his fingers onto the cap and opened the bottle. When he was about to take a sip, a poster boy from behind slapped and kicked him so rigorously with intentions and the bottle watered the ground and dropped off his meek hands. But the wanderer took the moment and picked up the bottle once again and started to drink but again the boy stole the moment and again nagged him. The bottle was then completely on the ground emptied. The wanderer never lost his hope and started once again barefooted along the natural stores.

Wanderer's encounter with the Poster Boys

The park was full of nasty poster boys as if they represents dignified roles. What's the difference between the boys and the wanderer? Nevertheless, the situations were the same. The wanderer on the lines found a pair of tattered boots and said to him,
"Oh, God thank you...I can't wait to wear them. You are merciful. The people who threw them in the name of rituals should be blessed. As their rituals gave me suffice in my nothingness."
He wore them with a struggle and started once again with a spirit. He was happy. Moving his eyes to the fullest and granting everything a blessing. He took everything optimistically and paused his chaotic thoughts. While a walk, she saw a beggar woman sleeping under the shade of a tree having a bag of garbage beside her. He searched that quietly and found a bottle filled with water and an emptied bottle with the same.........

*II*

He moved once again on a trip to nowhere. He meets two boys who teased him. They took his bag and threw it on the ground. One of them checked the pockets of his tattered jeans for money and the other one started beating him off with a stick. They both caught him and snatched his spirit. He broke up with his situation and lamented his date while beaten up. Suddenly, one boy was watching them from behind the bushes and was startled by the sight to guard that helpless spirit. He poked in between and saved him and they both eloped in s scene. Both were into their laughs and shrieks and disappeared..........
The boy took the wanderer into generosity and brought him relief. He said,
"Come with me, will render to some food"
"Sure, you are saying."
They both walked along to a tree nearby and sat. The boy offered him a polybag full of fruits and snacks and an address slip while talking to him about the task.
"You have to follow this to reach the bank."
"Like for what?"
"To rob the authorities of the bank and be careful.....You have to do it. This is the address for a federal bank nearby. Take these bags and act on....."
"Will try."
The wanderer while following the address arrived at the address and went inside the bank. And in a few minutes, came back to the boy who was waiting for him in the same park. He came back with three bags full of notes and coins and gave back the bags to his master. He put the bags on the ground before him and started to quarrel.
"I want my share at least. I took a risk."
"Yes,.....Boys"
He called those poster boys and took all the wealth in his

possession and they started bearing them. Three of them worked
in connivance and misbehaved with the boy. And, left him in utter
despair after segregating their shares.
He was sitting lying back on the trunk of the tree and cursing his
deeds. He was flabbergasted and numbed. And said,
"Is this the life which is written for me? That emptied bottle is still
better than me at least, even a beggar can consider that for a drop
of water left at the bottom......Why am I feeling so dejected?........ Is
everything permanent or temporary in your court?"

Complaining about his Thirst and dejection


The day leaped all the hours and a new day began for him. He
started once again on the down lines in search of his needs and
found this time a bottle full of water and drank every with
content......

*Zillion children need love, the only desire they have but all they get in return is the wrath of the disastrous desires of humans in their multi-layered filthy faces.*

# DEJECTION - AN INFECTION

*Letter to Himself,*

*To My dearest Sons,*

*12<sup>th</sup> Of September, 1875*

*This hast to the visit to the alchemical practitioner and, he conferred two diabolical things; two things were of the knot of my conscience, and the news came forth to mold me into disheartenment. First and foremost, my only sons are connected medically and they are always with that only.......And if doctors perform surgery on them neither of them would die thereafter but the doctor consulted me that do this as this could be beneficial for one of your sons for his future. But, I just don't want to separate your soul and your flesh as by doing so you will be all alone, I want to see you when I depart from this mortal cage by my twain sons will not be suffering anymore......*

*Your Loving Father,*

Jack Martin

# I

I read this letter as my morning prayer, now things have converted from caterpillar to butterflies, seasons have passed and the hatchlings have grown wings flying high and, new flowers bloomed on the carcass of their parental flesh. There is no foundation of our hamlet where we twain brothers work and reside.

"Oh! Back, son of Jack doesn't try to pluck those flowers, they have thorns to protect."

"Oh! Lack your conscience always lack don't worry I am your back just let me have that flower as today is the 25<sup>th</sup> death anniversary of our father, Jack."

Suddenly, Back screamed in agony as his index finger was kissed by a rosed throne. Back consoled him and put his finger in his mouth and sucked his blood. Lack answered in tears,

"You have my back, don't worry it's just a romance with a rose band. You will be fine."

" Oh Back, you know how much I am weak, that's just felt so intriguing."

Daily, they both enjoyed their spaces and never felt alone. They were always together in struggles and follies. Regularly they were visiting their father's graveyard and remembered him as the only letter left by him which he had penned down in these cancerous days. They loved their father a lot. Jack always inspired him no matter if he never meet them in reality.........

And, then a night came which often comes with an aftermath full of dejection. Lack was cunningly preparing the pipe of opium, but as the moonlight breaks the darkness, every cunning act has an audience all around.

"Why do you do this lack? I don't think you lack in wisdom, and I don't think you lack in faith, so why you're towards me starting lacking, too want to leave me as Father did? Oh! Benevolent souls cursed that desirous boy who puked his desires into my brother's veins and I am here sobbing thinking of the aftermath which I have to face all alone."

"Oh! That's not lack, I am fond of having opium as I can't escape this...Pardon me, don't get rid of me at least."

"You always do this, I am frustrated, please don't talk with me."

This was habitual to them, back always took opium, and lack got annoyed him. Back always offered him his favorite dish, Lamb Meat as his tactic to treat him. Lack as agreed to back's wishes. As this was no new to them, that happened daily. On one random day, when they both were as usual at their father's grave. One couple was romancing and kissing which they both noticed but back changed lack's sight and diverted him to a blooming flower. Lack is always a meek boy who even can't handle a cauldron with his one hand.


## II


By visiting my place daily, you will not get back your brother again, the doctor answered to lack.

"I lack my soul now, he was not just my half flesh, he was also my half soul. I have no back now at least you should have thought something before that doctor."

"But, this is not my fault, though you both were connected by flesh and soul still. Back's body weight and sensitivity were more on his part and you are interior to strength and ligaments...I can't do this now it's not in my hands to save either by any choice."

"What's just fallen upon me this dejection...I don't have my back now."

"No, that's in your spine, just feel him in you in your flesh and soul. Make this dejection your medicine, not make it your infection."

Lack was then alone on his way to the places where he was used to being. The places they had been before being to the waterfalls, the blooming gardens, and the graveyard. The back's grave was then along his father's grave. Once when he was near the water stream, lack called him to play with pebbles which they used to throw into the waters but suddenly realized that was his vision of him. He came to the waters, suddenly Jack hold him from behind and back from the front, they hugged tightly for a while in between Lack's fingers touched one another. With a meandering breeze of air, he came up to his wisdom and realized that no one was there except memories. He paused for a while and started murmuring,

"I now understand the merry place of the merciful playwright. I always wished for a cure for my opium habit. He erased all my desires and cured me at the cost of losing my soul. My soul is enacted with infection now so oh merciful playwright heal my soul again before gangrene takes the rest."

Lack returned to his house and as he opened the door, he saw
Back in the room calling him to play hide and seek as they used to
play when at home. Lack closed his eyes and started counting
1...2...3...4...and as he said 10, he started searching Back in every
corner of the house. The surroundings then made him realize and
he started crying. He found himself as the only person in the
deserted house. Screaming in agony, crying, and crying in utter
dejection.......

*To whom you love, you always mark their sayings no
matter if you have to change your habits or your
desires for that. And, if you don't bother about their
words, it means you don't love them because when
you love someone, their every utterance is like the
oxygen you breathe and without breath, you cannot
survive.*

# Upcoming Titles

**JUST IN A WHILE and**

**BARFING OUT PUTRID TOOLS OF THE TORSO** - The two individual poetic collections.

**TROVE OF THOUGHTS - SECTION II**

**A Mock Epic - ***UNTITLED*****

**A Novel as Prequel To The Modern Faustus**